Susan Mu...

illustrations by E...

MORE
BLUEBERRIES!

ORCA BOOK PUBLISHERS

Text copyright © 2015 Susan Musgrave
Illustrations copyright © 2015 Esperança Melo

**Cataloguing in Publication information available
from Library and Archives Canada**

Issued in print and electronic formats.
ISBN 978-1-4598-1505-6 (paperback).—
ISBN 978-1-4598-0708-2 (pdf).—ISBN 978-1-4598-0709-9 (epub)

First published in the United States, 2017
Library of Congress Control Number: 2016949039

Summary: In this rhyming picture book for preschoolers, young
twins can't get enough of their favorite fruit.

MIX
Paper from
responsible sources
FSC® C013314

*Orca Book Publishers is dedicated to preserving the environment and has
printed this book on Forest Stewardship Council® certified paper.*

Orca Book Publishers gratefully acknowledges the support
for its publishing programs provided by the following agencies:
the Government of Canada through the Canada Book Fund and the
Canada Council for the Arts, and the Province of British Columbia
through the BC Arts Council and the Book Publishing Tax Credit.

Interior and cover artwork created using acrylic on gessoed paper.

Cover artwork by Esperança Melo
Design by Chantal Gabriell and Esperança Melo

ORCA BOOK PUBLISHERS
www.orcabook.com

Printed and bound in China.

20 19 18 17 • 4 3 2 1

Blueberry cheeks,
blueberry chin.

Blueberry teeth,
blueberry grin.

Blueberry fingers,
blueberry nose.

Blueberry lips,
blueberry toes.

Yummy! Tasty!

MORE

BLUEBERRIES!

Blueberry pancakes,
blueberry mush.
Blueberry muffins,
blueberry slush.

Blueberry ice cream,
blueberry cake.
Blueberry tummy,
blueberry ACHE.

Slurp! Burp!

MORE

BLUEBERRIES!

Cats chase blueberries,
then lick their paws.
When crows find blueberries—

caw!

caw!

CAW!

Frogs hop on blueberries,
pop, HOP, pop.

When bears gobble blueberries,
blueberry PLOP.

Meow. CAW. Ribbit. Grrrrrrrr.

MORE
BLUEBE

Blueberry bathtime,
blueberry MESS.
Blueberry pants,
blueberry dress.

Blueberry jammies,
blueberry yawn.
Blueberry bedtime,
blueberries gone.